Fun with Paper

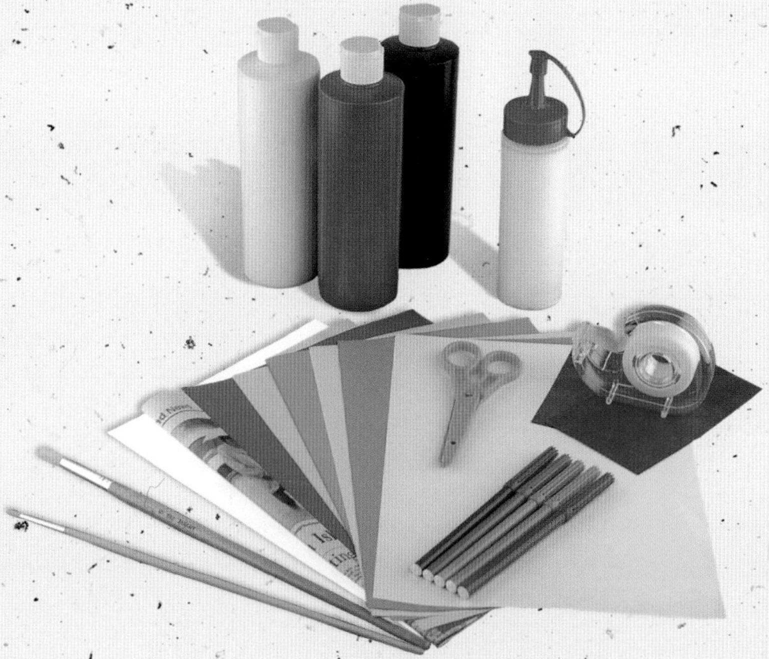

Written by Sylvia Lee

I made a paper hat.

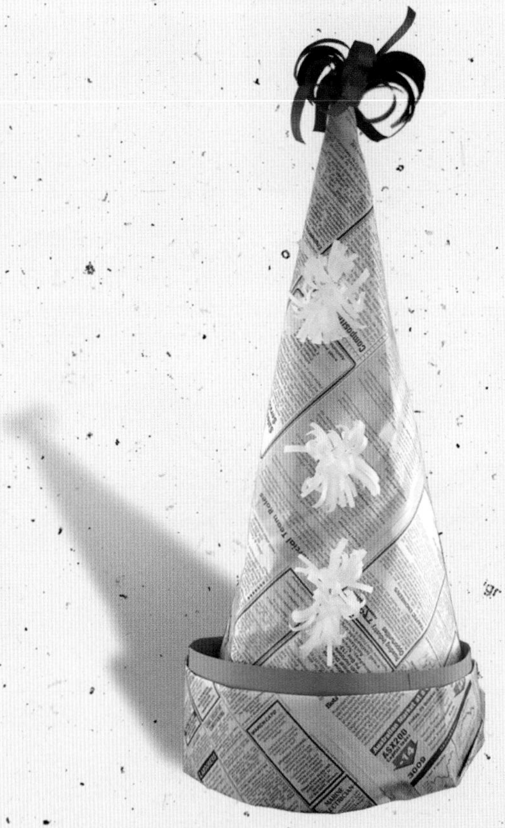

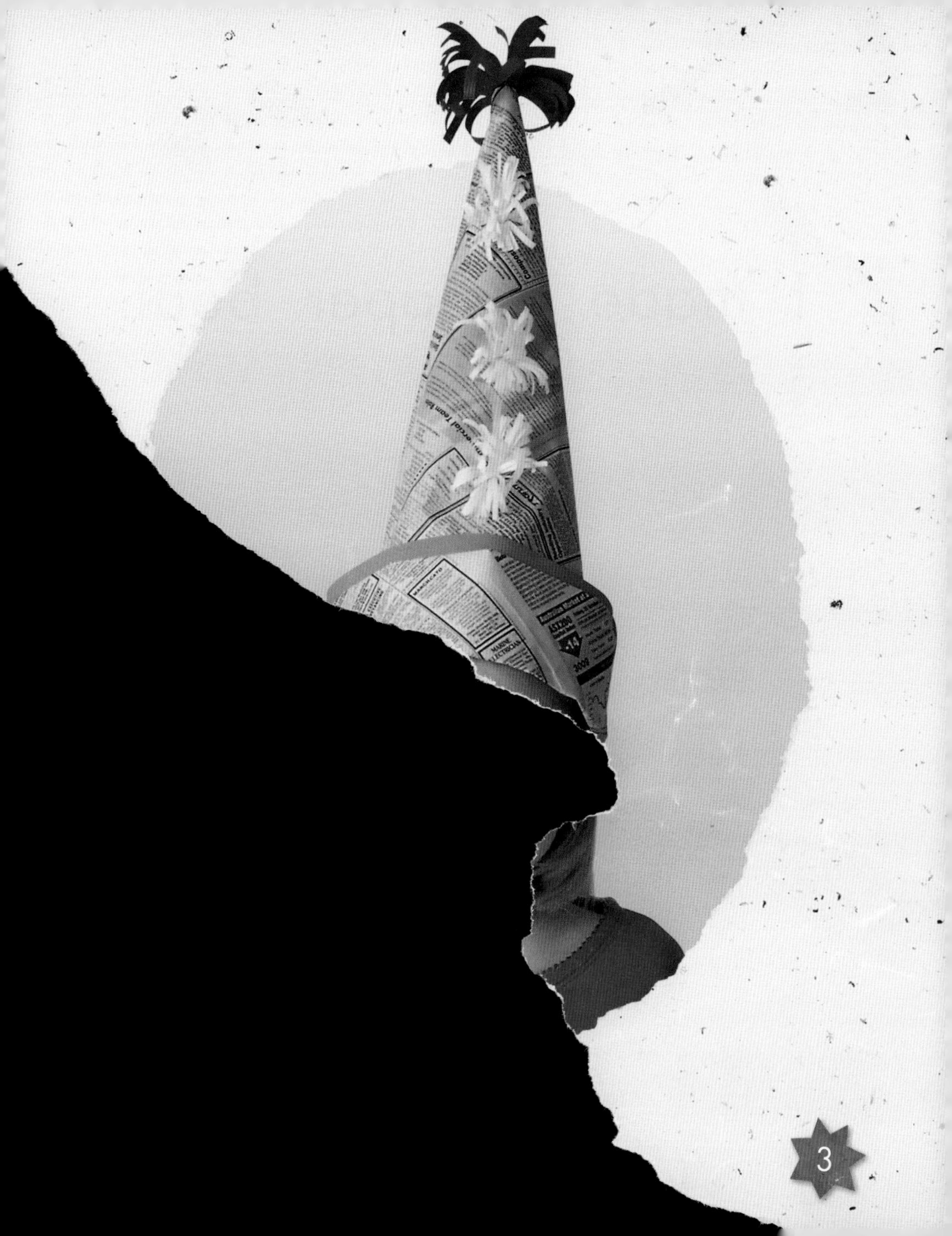

I made a paper boat.

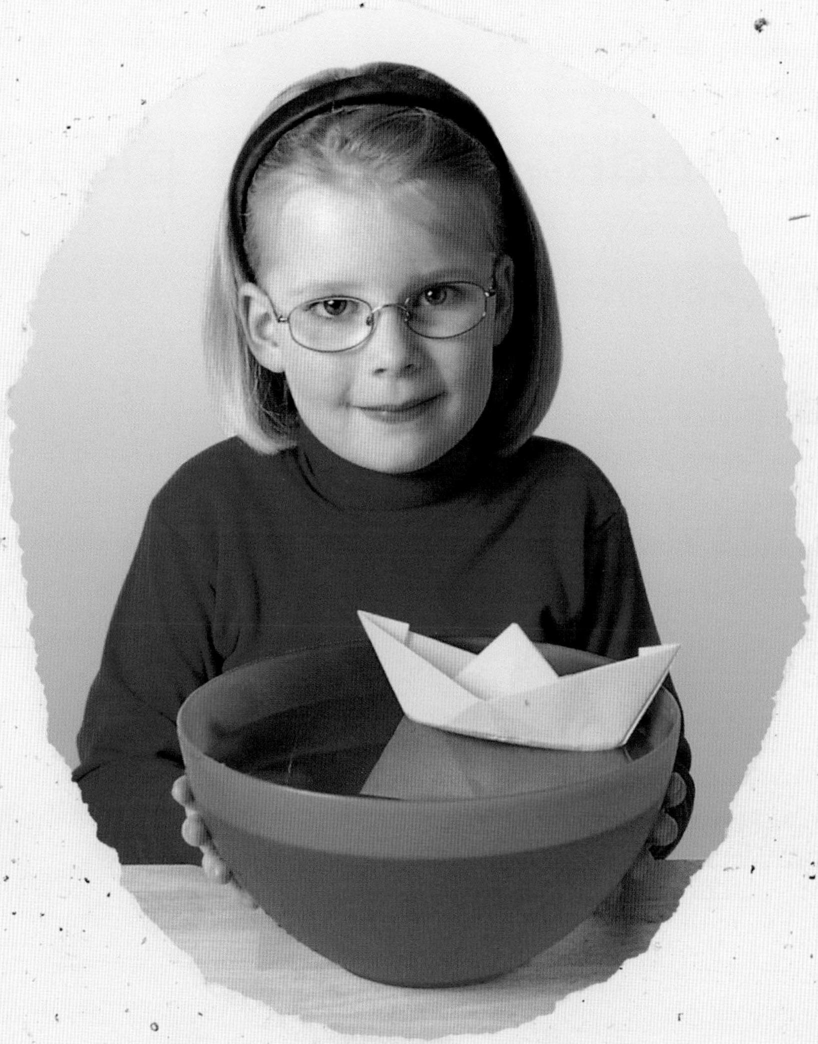

I made a paper plane.

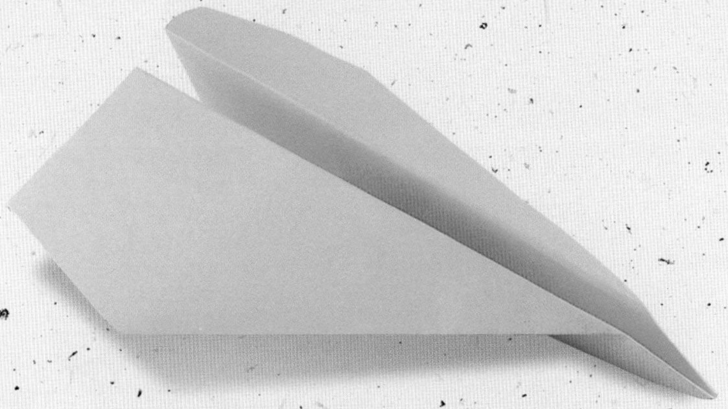

I made a paper mask.

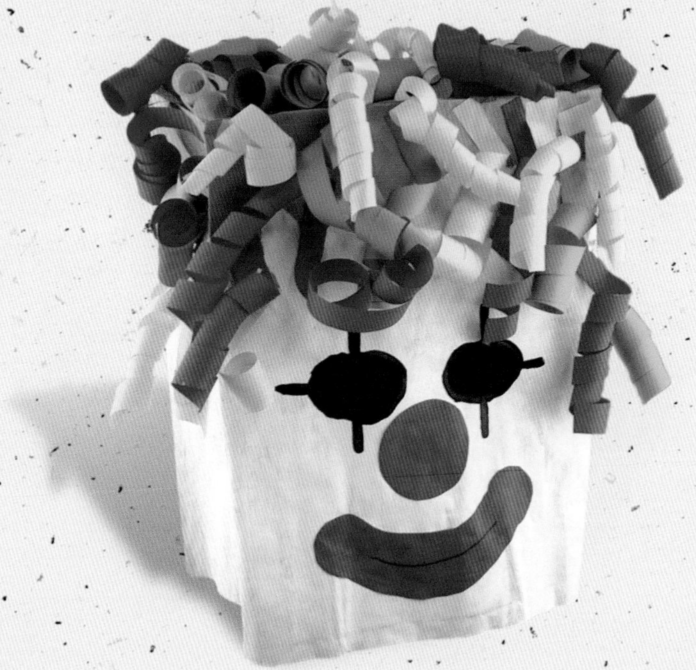

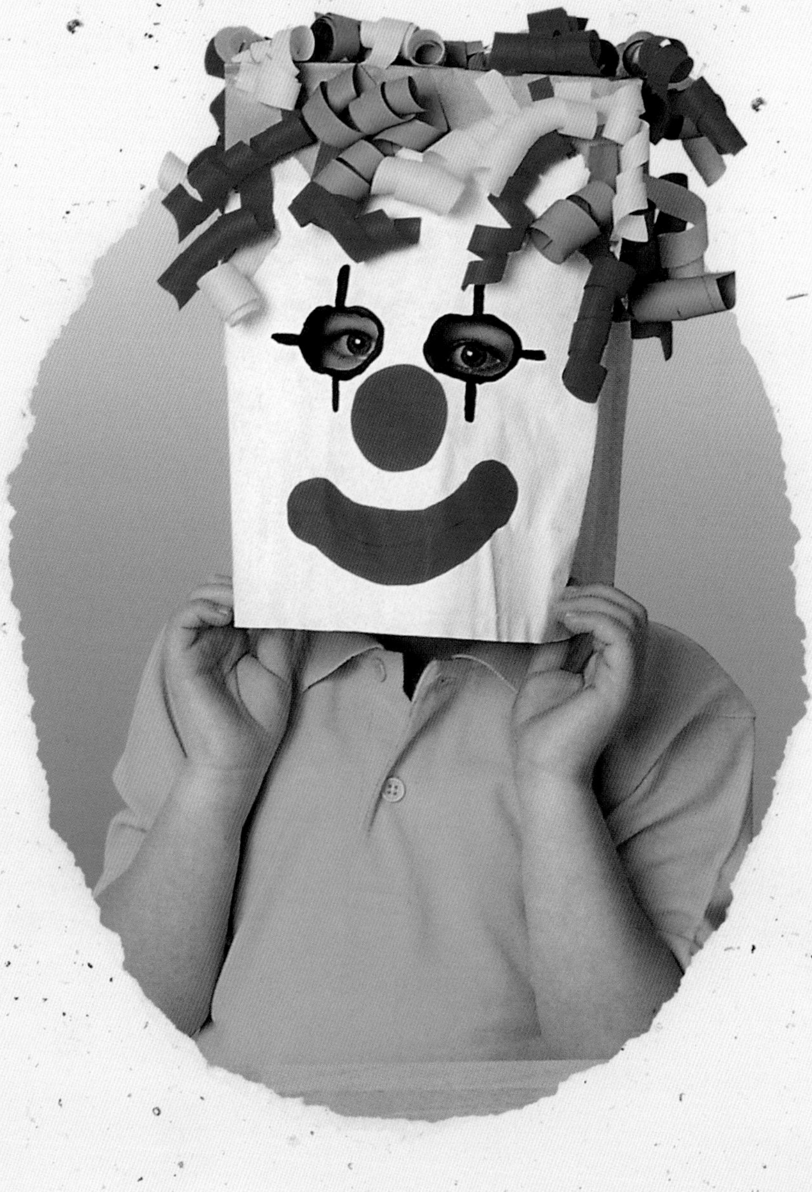

I made a paper puppet.

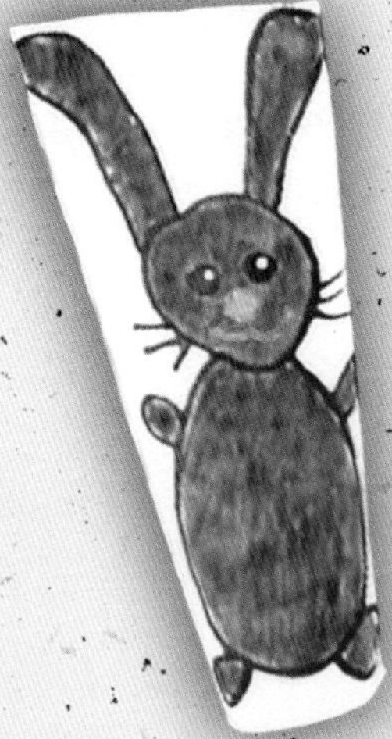

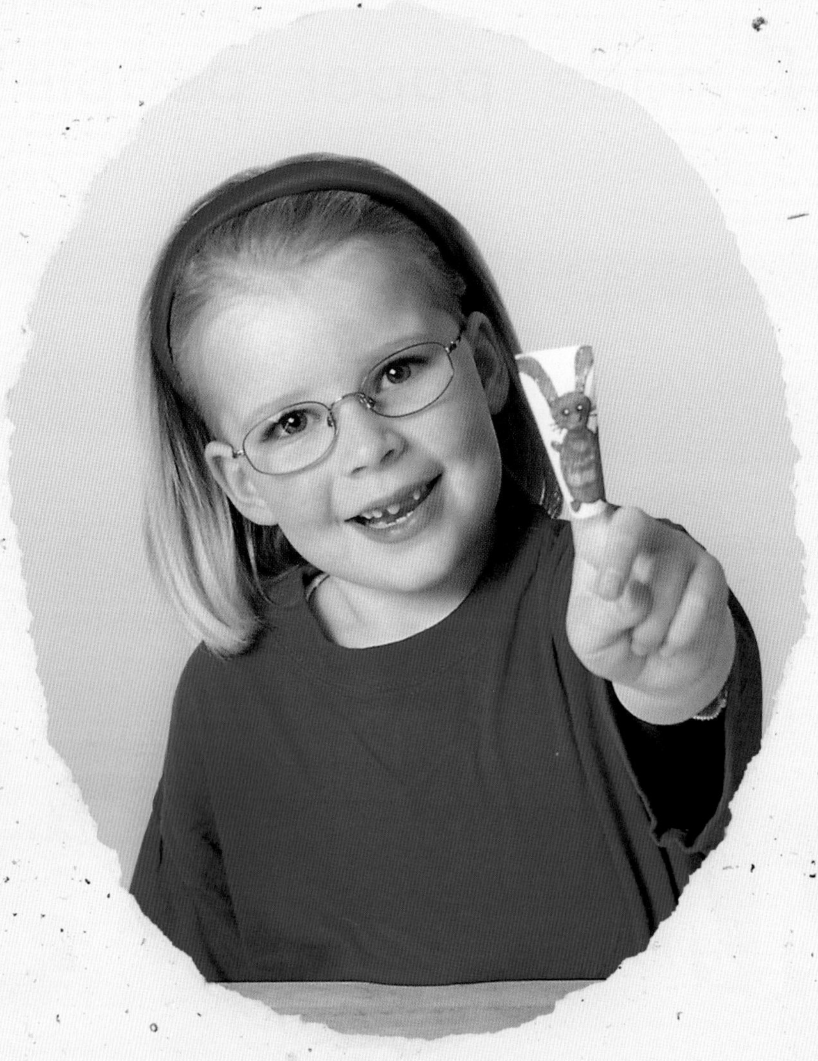

I made paper people!

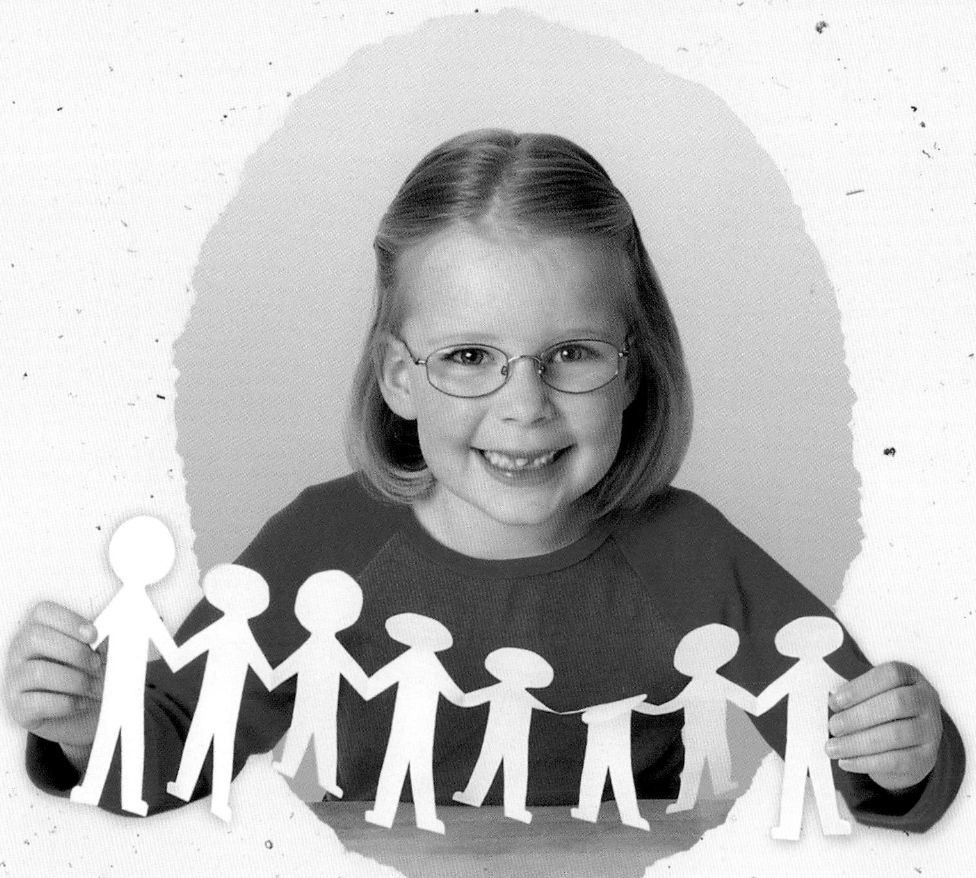